JACK KENT

SOCKS for SUPPER

Parents' Magazine Press · New York

Copyright © 1978 by Jack Kent
All rights reserved
Printed in the United States of America
10   9   8   7   6   5   4   3   2   1

Library of Congress Cataloging in Publication Data
Kent, Jack, 1920-
    The sock exchange.
    SUMMARY: When a poor couple exchange socks for
cheese and milk, they receive more than expected.
    [1. Friendship—Fiction]   I.   Title.
PZ7.K414So   [E]   78-6224
ISBN 0-8193-0964-8   ISBN 0-8193-0965-6 lib. bdg.

SOCKS FOR SUPPER

In a faraway place in a long-ago time
there lived an old man and his wife.
They were very poor.

All they had was a tumble-down house
and a tiny turnip garden.

One day, he said to his wife,
"One can get tired of eating
nothing but turnips."

Not far away there lived a couple
who had a cow.
The old man and his wife
used to look at the cow
 and dream of milk and cheese.

"Maybe they'll sell us some,"
said the old man.
"We don't have any money,"
his wife reminded him.
"Perhaps we could trade them
something for some milk,"
said the old man.

"Perhaps we could," his wife agreed.
And they searched the house for
something to trade.
They looked and looked
but the only thing they could find
that wasn't in pieces or tatters
was a pair of socks.

The old man took the socks
and went to see the couple
who had the cow.

A little while later
he came happily home again
with a bucket of milk
and a small cheese.

"Oh! This is so good!" said his wife.

It wasn't long before they began
to wish they had some more. But they
didn't have any more socks to trade.

"I will knit some!" said the old woman.

But she didn't have any yarn.

So she unraveled part of the old man's
sweater and knitted a pair of socks
with that.

They again traded the socks for
milk and cheese.

And they feasted as they did before.

When it was all gone, the old woman
knitted another pair of socks.

And once more the old man
traded them for milk and cheese.

YUM!

When that was gone, the old woman
started knitting again.

But there was now only enough yarn
left for one sock.

"What good is one sock?"
the old woman asked. "They won't trade
any milk or cheese for that"

"We'll see," said the old man.
And he took the sock
to the couple with the cow.

"I only have half a pair of socks
this time," he said. "Would you trade
half a bucket of milk
and half a cheese for this?"

"Oh, no, that is not necessary," said the farmer.

"You see," said the farmer's wife,
"One sock is exactly what I need."

She was knitting her husband a sweater
for Christmas. She'd gotten the yarn
for it by unraveling the socks and she
needed just one more to finish the job.

But the sweater didn't fit.

So the wife gave it to the old man,
for she had noticed he didn't have one.

And it was just the right size.